Gold medal winner of
the Key Colors Competition USA, 2020

My Key written and illustrated by Amal

ISBN 978-1-60537-689-9

This book was printed in July 2021 at Drukarnia Perfekt S. A., ul. Połczyńska 99, 01-303 Warszawa, Poland.

First Edition
10 9 8 7 6 5 4 3 2 1

Amal

My Key

Clavis

NEW YORK

I asked politely, *"Please* can we go to the movies, Timbuktu, a little kasbah in a big city?
You know, one of those old Moroccan fortresses. *Please?"* Mama said she'd take me to the library, but maybe later.
"Maybe *now?"* I asked. She said it again, *"Maybe* later."
Can you believe it, Tiberius? *Maybe* was the answer I got yesterday too.
Meow . . .

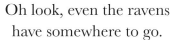

Oh look, even the ravens
have somewhere to go.

Hey, what do you suppose
those are, Tiberius?

This ball is warm.
And I swear it's smiling at me.

Excuse me, Tiberius.
Don't worry, stand back,
this is *not* a normal ball.
As a matter of fact . . .
Meow!

Whoa! It beams!
It's fantastic!
Adios, Mama!
My Fantastic Beaming Ball
says we'll be home before dark.

Are we sailing to that palace?
The water is strange, everything is too quiet,
and I hear the slithering sounds of . . .

. . . sea monsters!
Hurry, Fantastic Beaming Ball!
Pilot us out of here before
these creatures gobble us whole.

No! You can't have my ball. It won't do anything for you!

Trust me, it really won't.

It only shines for me, you know!

Captain and Fantastic Beaming Ball
traveling to a palace over calm seas.

Of course! The LIBRARY!

A palace of books!
There's a lot of exploring to do.

Are you kidding?

LIBRARY

CLOSED TODAY

FOR

VERY IMPORTANT

YOUNG ELEPHANT

BOOK CONFERENCE

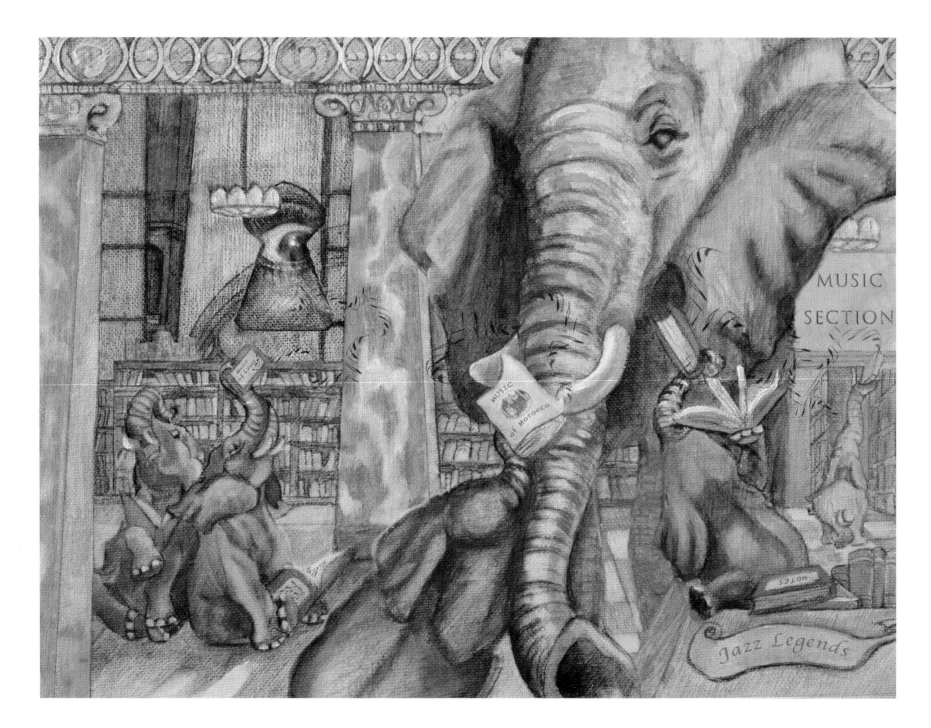

One way or another, I'm getting inside.

I can make myself a key, unlock the door, and turn *maybe* into . . .

One big YES! Time for exploration.

More than one way . . .   . . . to reach . . .   . . . a kasbah.

Hey, little fellow! Do elephant trunks pop out of books at all your conferences?

WHOOSH . . . . I'm getting sucked in . . . . Where am I going ?

Where am I going ? . . . . I'm getting sucked in . . . . WHOOSH

I knew I'd get to Morocco!

Down there!
Look, it's like the kasbah
I saw in my library book!

What have you got there, little friend?

This kasbah is far too quiet. Hand me all your sticks and balls and you'll see what I'll make happen.

What? A jam session? All night? That's crazy.

I'm a bat. Nighttime is *my* time!

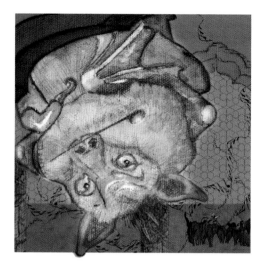

This girl has
gone far enough.
I insist on . . .

QUIET!

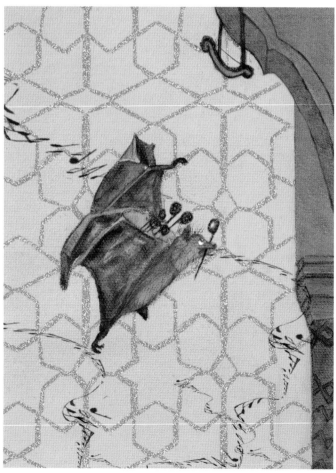

Gotcha!

Don't cry, little fellow, me and my key can fix anything.
You can have a jam session every night! Or, *maybe*, every day.

Thank you, little fellow.
You say there's a chameleon conference in thirteen minutes?
One quick peek at my gift before I leave . . .

Tiberius? Is that you?

I'm back! Can you help me with this book, please?

Thanks, and I'll see you all tomorrow.

Okay, Tiberius, what do you think about dinosaurs?
Because next trip, you're coming with me.
Meow?